W9-BXZ-189

Margaret Hillert's

Four Good Friends

A Beginning-to-Read Book

Illustrated by Roberta Collier—Morales
retold story of The Bremen Town Musicians

NORWOOD HOUSE PRESS

DEAR CAREGIVER,

The books in this Beginning-to-Read collection may look somewhat familiar in that the original versions could have been a part of your own early reading experiences. These carefully written texts feature common sight words to provide your child multiple exposures to the words appearing most frequently in written text. These new versions have been updated and the engaging illustrations are highly appealing to a contemporary audience of young readers.

Begin by reading the story to your child, followed by letting him or her read familiar words and soon your child will be able to read the story independently. At each step of the way, be sure to praise your reader's efforts to build his or her confidence as an independent reader. Discuss the pictures and encourage your child to make connections between the story and his or her own life. At the end of the story, you will find reading activities and a word list that will help your child practice and strengthen beginning reading skills. These activities, along with the comprehension questions are aligned to current standards, so reading efforts at home will directly support the instructional goals in the classroom.

Above all, the most important part of the reading experience is to have fun and enjoy it!

Shannon Cannon

Shannon Cannon,
Literacy Consultant

Norwood House Press • www.norwoodhousepress.com
Beginning-to-Read™ is a registered trademark of Norwood House Press.
Illustration and cover design copyright ©2017 by Norwood House Press. All Rights Reserved.

Authorized adapted reprint from the U.S. English language edition, entitled Four Good Friends by Margaret Hillert. Copyright © 2017 Margaret Hillert. Reprinted with permission. All rights reserved. Pearson and Four Good Friends are trademarks, in the US and/or other countries, of Pearson Education, Inc. or its affiliates. This publication is protected by copyright, and prior permission to re-use in any way in any format is required by both Norwood House Press and Pearson Education. This book is authorized in the United States for use in schools and public libraries.

Designer: Lindaanne Donohoe
Editorial Production: Lisa Walsh

LIBRARY OF CONGRESS CATALOGING-IN-PUBLICATION DATA
Names: Hillert, Margaret, author. | Collier-Morales, Roberta, illustrator.
Title: Four good friends / by Margaret Hillert ; illustrated by Roberta Collier-Morales.
Description: Chicago, IL : Norwood House Press, 2016. | Series: A
  Beginning-to-read book | Summary: "An easy format retelling of the classic
  fairytale, Bremen Town Musicians and their search for a place to live.
  Original edition revised with new illustrations. Includes reading
  activities and a word list"-- Provided by publisher.
Identifiers: LCCN 2015047780 (print) | LCCN 2016009491 (ebook) | ISBN
  9781599537801 (library edition : alk. paper) | ISBN 9781603579216 (eBook)
Subjects: | CYAC: Fairy tales. | Folklore--Germany.
Classification: LCC PZ8.H5425 Fo 2016 (print) | LCC PZ8.H5425 (ebook) | DDC
  398.2--dc23
LC record available at http://lccn.loc.gov/2015047780

288N—072016
Manufactured in the United States of America in North Mankato, Minnesota.

I can not work.
No one wants me.
I have to go away.
Away, away, away.

Oh, my. Oh, my.
You do not look good, little one.
Why?
What is it?

I can not work.
No one wants me.
I am no good.

Come. Come.
I like you.
You can come with me.

See here now.
We will go away.
We will find something.

What is this?
What have we here?
You are a big one.

I can not run.
I can not work.
What will I do now?
Where will I go?

You are big.
Big, big, big.
You can help us.

You can come with us.
We want you.
Come with us to see
what we can find.

My, how pretty you are.
But, what is it?
Can we help?

I am no good,
I guess.
No one wants me.
What am I to do?

Do you want to come with us?
We like you.
We want you.

Look here.
A little house.
Is this what we want?

Have a look.
What do you see?
What is in this house?

I see a man.
I see two.
I see three.

We want to see, too.
Do it like this.
Here we go.
Up and up and up.

Oh, oh, oh!
Oh, my. Oh, my!
Oh, look at that!

Get out! Get out!
It is not good for us here.
Get away! Get away!
Run, run, run.

Now that is funny.
What did we do?
But come in here.
It looks good in here.

Now we have a house.
We have something
to eat.
We can not work.
But we are happy.

Foundational Skills

In addition to reading the numerous high-frequency words in the text, this book also supports the development of foundational skills.

Phonological Awareness: The /f/ sound

Oral Blending: Say the beginning sounds listed below and ask your child to say the word formed by adding the **/f/** sound to the end:

roo + /f/ = roof	lea + /f/ = leaf	che + /f/ = chef
hu + /f/ = huff	li + /f/ = life	wol + /f/ = wolf
loa + /f/ = loaf	bee + /f/ = beef	el + /f/ = elf
shel + /f/ = shelf	kni + /f/ = knife	scar + /f/ = scarf

Phonics: The letter Ff

1. Demonstrate how to form the letters **F** and **f** for your child.
2. Have your child practice writing **F** and **f** at least three times each.
3. Ask your child to point to the words in the book that begin with the letter **f**.
4. Write down the following words and ask your child to circle the letter **f** in each word:

for	fun	raft	fur	foot
fast	roof	if	sift	friend
fold	lift	fluff	flat	stuff

Fluency: Shared Reading

1. Reread the story to your child at least two more times while your child tracks the print by running a finger under the words as they are read. Ask your child to read the words he or she knows with you.
2. Reread the story taking turns, alternating readers between sentences or pages.

Language

The concepts, illustrations, and text help children develop language both explicitly and implicitly.

Vocabulary: Synonyms

1. Write the following words on separate pieces of paper:

small	scared	house	thin	joyful
big	slender	nice	happy	afraid
little	excellent	tired	run	make
sleepy	jog	large	create	pretty
good	home	lovely	great	

2. Read each word to your child and ask your child to repeat it.
3. Explain to your child that when two different words mean almost the same thing, they are called synonyms.
4. Mix the words up. Point to a word and ask your child to read it. Provide clues if your child needs them. Ask your child to match the pairs of synonym words.

Reading Literature and Informational Text

To support comprehension, ask your child the following questions. The answers either come directly from the text or require inferences and discussion.

Key Ideas and Detail

• Ask your child to retell the sequence of events in the story.
• What did the four friends have in common?

Craft and Structure

• Is this a book that tells a story or one that gives information? How do you know?
• How did the animals help each other?

Integration of Knowledge and Ideas

• Why do you think the men left the house?
• Can you describe a time when you felt bad but everything turned out okay?

WORD LIST

Four Good Friends uses the 63 words listed below.

This list can be used to practice reading the words that appear in the text. You may wish to write the words on index cards and use them to help your child build automatic word recognition. Regular practice with these words will enhance your child's fluency in reading connected text.

a	eat	I	oh	up
am		in	one	us
and	find	is	out	
are	for	it		want(s)
at	funny		pretty	we
away		like		what
	get	little	run	where
big	go	look(s)		why
but	good		see	will
	guess	man	something	with
can		me		work
come	happy	my	that	
	have		this	you
did	help	no	three	
do	here	not	to	
	house	now	too	
	how		two	

ABOUT THE AUTHOR   Margaret Hillert has helped millions of children all over the world learn to read independently. She was a first grade teacher for 34 years and during that time started writing books that her students could both gain confidence in reading and enjoy. She wrote well over 100 books for children just learning to read. As a child, she enjoyed writing poetry and continued her poetic writings as an adult for both children and adults.

Photograph by Glenna Washburn

ABOUT THE ILLUSTRATOR   Roberta Collier-Morales has been illustrating children's books, educational materials, mass market, and religious subjects for over 33 years. She creates art for fabric and fine art prints. She works in a studio with a view of the mountains in Colorado with her two dogs, two cats, three goldfish, son and mom. www.robertacolliermorales.com